Let's Play
MOVING HOME
Written and illustrated by
Rosella Badessa and Roberto Rizzon

Child's Play (International) Ltd
Swindon   Auburn ME   Sydney

© 1999 M. Twinn   ISBN 0-85953-712-9   Printed in India

Are you all in your groups?

Get moving!

Look behind you, Little Fish!

Little Fish, behind you!

Little Fish, below you!

Well done, Little Fish!

Who is in the middle now?

Little Bird, look below you!

Little Bird, look up!

Little Bird, be quick!

Welcome home, Little Bird.   Who is in the middle now?

Beetle, look up!

Beetle, look down!

Beetle, look behind you!

Well done, Beetle!   But who will be in the middle?

Below you, Owl!

Above you, Owl!

Above you, Owl!

Who is in the middle now?   Thank you, Chimpanzee.

Look over here, Penguin!

Look behind you, Penguin!

Mind you don't slip, Penguin! Whoops!

Well swum, Penguin!   Who is in the middle now?

It's nice to see new places, but there's no place like home.